For Better or For Worse:®

Another Day, Another Lecture

Lynn Johnston

TOR

A TOM DOHERTY ASSOCIATES BOOK
NEW YORK

This is a work of fiction. All the characters and events portrayed in this book are fictitious, and any resemblance to real people or events is purely coincidental.

FOR BETTER OR FOR WORSE®: ANOTHER DAY, ANOTHER LECTURE

FOR BETTER OR FOR WORSE® is a registered trademark of Lynn Johnston. All rights reserved.

Copyright © 1991 by Lynn Johnston, distributed internationally by Universal Press Syndicate.

No part of this book may be used or reproduced in any manner whatsoever without written permission except in the case of reprints in the context of reviews. For information write: Andrews & McMeel, a Universal Press Syndicate Affiliate, 4900 Main Street, Kansas City, Missouri, 64112.

A Tor Book
Published by Tom Doherty Associates, Inc.
49 West 24th Street
New York, N.Y. 10010

ISBN: 0-812-51736-9

First Tor edition: December 1991

Printed in the United States of America

0 9 8 7 6 5 4 3 2 1

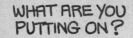

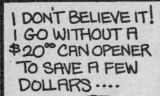

THE HOUSE IS SURE QUIET WHEN A KID IS SICK.

SNIFF

THIS IS THE ONE TIME I PREFER THE NOISE.

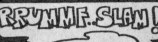

LIZZIE. AS OF TODAY... YOU ARE OFFICIALLY TOO BIG FOR THE BACK-PACK.

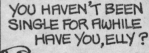

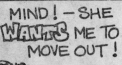

I'M LOOKING FORWARD TO THIS VACATION AND HAVING TIME TOGETHER, ELLY.

AS WELL AS BEING PARENTS, I WANT THE KIDS TO SEE US AS REAL, BASIC HUMAN BEINGS!

HONEY, IF 2 WEEKS IN THE BUSH WITH A WOOD STOVE AND AN OUTHOUSE WON'T DO IT...

NOTHING WILL.

LYNN

THE LOCK IS RUSTED SHUT, SO I'VE TAKEN THE DOOR OFF THE BOAT HOUSE.
WOW! - A CANOE, DADDY - A CANOE!
NOW, THERE'S A SPECIAL WAY OF GETTING INTO A CANOE, MICHAEL....
DON'T JUST STAND THERE! GO ASK YOUR MOTHER WHAT IT IS!!